The Naughty List

Prince Albert King

Copyright © 2022 Dr. Prince Albert King™

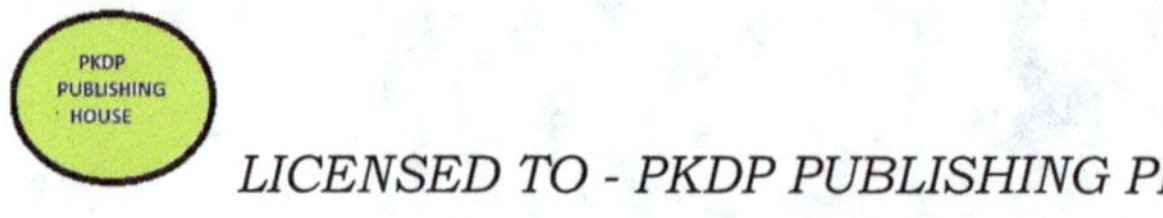

LICENSED TO - PKDP PUBLISHING PRESS

EMAIL: pkdpsales@gmail.com

www.authorpaking@gmail.com

P.O.BOX SB51712 NASSAU,

NEWPROVIDENCE THE BAHAMAS

All rights reserved.

From The series: The Adventures of

Motlee the Butterfly

For kids 2-9 years old

Illustrated by: PKDP PRESS

Motlee the Butterfly —

A kid's fictional Christmas story

<u>Acknowledgements:</u>

Art director:

Graphics artist: creative fabrica &

Vecteezy.com

Story editor:

Script coordinator:

Character designer:

From The Author:

Prince Albert King & PKDP has Lots of Pages for the Kids and is created right in time for the holidays, Parents and Kids Ages 2-9 will love it we can help your child self-regulate their emotions and actions. The series contains little stories about Big feelings teaches emotional control and how to effectively act when faced with overwhelming emotions or challenging circumstances

Focusing on four primary emotions: anger, sadness, frustration, and happiness children will learn to welcome their feelings and listen to them instead of impulsively reacting. Managing big emotions can help children act effectively and solve conflict independently while working their way back to a calm, happy state.

Series: Adventures of Motley and Humbert by Prince Albert King.

The Book is the first book in its series and follows the theme of helping children find their inner bravery by navigating change, transitions, and new feelings.

The BIG Emotions emphasized are:

Anger: *An intense, heightened emotion can often be overwhelming to children and can lead to adverse reactions when they do not understand the reason why they feel this way. When in a state of anger, children need to learn to stop and breathe before reacting. That control is possible with practice. That calming and self-soothing oneself is an essential first step in managing or controlling this emotion. Motley in the story becomes angry because 1. He did not get a gift from Santa 2.He did not get things to go his way. Kids need to know that in life things do not always go the way we want it .This is true even for adults too.* **Sadness:** *An emotional pain associated with feelings of loss, despair, grief,* *helplessness, and disappointment. Sadness can be especially hard for a child when they don't have comfort or understanding of why their feeling this way or that it's simply OK to feel sad sometimes.*

Frustration: *An emotional response to conflict or opposition. Frustration can often occur from being unable to solve a problem, experiencing a roadblock, or annoyance. Frustration in a child can often lead to anger and adverse reactions if one does not take caution. Stopping to take a break and breathe is often a great way to prevent irritation.*

Happiness: *An emotional state or feelings of satisfaction, joy, and fulfillment. When a child is happy, they are often calm and be ready to learn. Teaching children techniques like breathing, stopping, and realizing the core of their feelings is a critical way to get back to feeling happy. The characters were happy with their rewards for* *their help and kindness a sleigh ride and the title of honoree Elves.*

***Restitution** is **the act of making up for damages or harm done**. Remember the time you knocked the ball out of the park, scoring a home run but breaking a house's window in the process? You had to make restitution for the broken window, paying for its replacement. The Characters in this story book had to make restitution for the wrong that they did and they went the extra mile by helping Santa in other ways after undoing what they had done before.*

Through the PKDP Kid Press book series, your child will learn:

The importance of trying something new.

How to self-regulate BIG emotions.

That bravery, courage and strength lies within and we can access it at any time.

Overcoming new challenges can often lead to even more fun and adventure!

The importance of consistency. Grit and perseverance help challenges become easier with time.

The incredible feeling of conquering hard things!

That kindness always wins.

It contains lovely illustrations and a storyline

It helps children recognize and cope with their anger in a real way through communication of positive affirmations.

It offers a calming technique and is aimed to improve kid's self-regulation skills

It teaches children to admit their mistakes. Forgive others and say "I'm sorry"

Table of Contents

Acknowledgements:

To: Samantha for reading and editing and reviewing this material, for assistance with the editing of the transcript material.

Canva

Vecteezy

Creative fabrica

Licensed to PKDP PUBLISHING HOUSE PRESS

Bahamas postal address: P.O.BOX SB51712

Email:pkdpsales@gmail.com

United States Postal address:

Prince King/Jetlocker-

5267 NW 161St. Ste.579B-Jl-OlaFot,

Miami Lakes. Florida, 33014.

CHAPTER 1 The life cycle of Motley And Humbert

Motley is a butterfly of the Monarch family. He entered the world as a little egg, that was laid onto a leave of a tree, then he was changed into a caterpillar and he ate himself fat. One day the caterpillar stopped eating and shed his skin. He had created a cocoon and after a period of hibernation twenty-one full days he was transformed into a butterfly.

Monarch Butterflies all go through four stages of changes or growth in a process called metamorphosis. It is like a transformation changing into something else. You can say that he is a real shapeshifter and transformer in one.

It just so happened that Motley came out of his cocoon on Christmas night. And so since Christmas had pass he looked forward to the next Christmas day. This was a double special day for him.

Motley tried very hard to be a good butterfly. He was doing wonderful until something happened to change all of that. Christmas day came and went but Motley did not enjoy it.

This made Motley very sad and frustrated. Sadness is not very pleasant. Frustration comes when someone cannot solve a problem.

No one likes to be sad or frustrated. It causes emotional pain associated with feelings of loss, despair, grief, helplessness, and disappointment. Motley, don't understand why he was feeling this way. He did not know that it was simply OK to feel sad sometimes. Everyone does. But we must not stay sad for too long. We all have the power inside of us to make ourselves happy again by changing our mood and thoughts quickly. We can

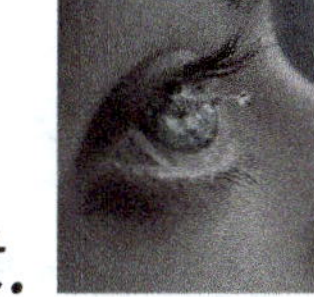

practice doing it.

Chapter 2 Nothing For Christmas

What is Christmas? Christmas is a well-known festival, a very popular holiday season worldwide. The festival is celebrated during the last week of the year on December 25 with gift giving. It is believed that Jesus Christ was born on this day. The festival is on December 25, but the celebrations start earlier and ends later with epiphany in different parts of the world.

Motley Had been overlooked on last Christmas by mistake. It was an oversight unforgiveable in Motley's eyes.

Santa Clause is to blame because he is in charge of the gifts, the Elves, the reindeers, the sleigh, even the North Pole workshop!" said Motley.

Motley did not know that Santa had been sick and the delivery was made by the chief elf instead last year.

All Motley knew was he and his friend Humbert got nothing for Christmas. They were good but somehow they made the naughty list.

Chapter 3 The Coming of Humbert

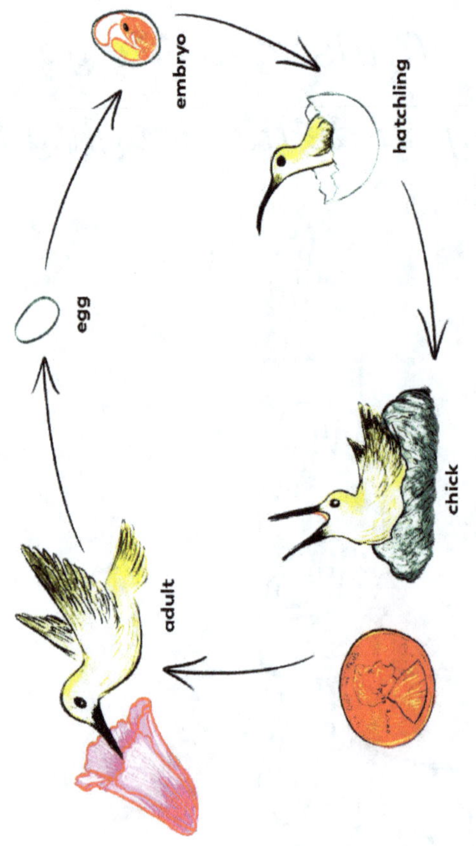

Papa bird had met mama bird one day as she entered his territory and they became mates.

It was during a migration event from North America to the sunny Isles of Nassau in the Bahamas.

A week later while flying for food, a hunter had caught papa bird in a trap.

The hunter had planned to use the bird for his little daughter Arianna as a pet.

He took the bird home to his little girl, the little girl was very happy to have a new pet.

But the mama bird would never see papa bird again. Mama bird would be alright however because she was built to be independent.

Mama Bird decided to choose a tree for her nesting. She began to build the nest from twigs and leaves in a tall almond tree.

She weaved together twigs, plant fibers, and bits of leaves, and used spider silk as threads to bind her nest together and anchor it to the foundation of the tree branch. The unique way of construction allows the nest to expand to contain the growing family. As such, the nests usually aren't suitable for reuse after it is expanded too much.

It took her seven days to finish the nest, although she would not be there forever, she took great pride in building her nest.

Humming birds usually have multiple broods each year, but they rarely reuse their nests. After they fledge the nest, they stay with their mother for around another 7 days, where she will continue to feed them.

After this time, at around 3-4 weeks old, the fledgling hummingbirds are developed enough and have practiced their flying skills enough to head off on their own.

Humming birds are the tiniest versions of the world's smallest birds, ornithologists call a newly hatched bird a nestling, hatchling, or chick.

Humbert hatch with his eyes closed and with almost no feathers.

Most hummingbird species live three to five years on average.

Mama bird laid two eggs and sat on them to keep the eggs warm. One day the eggs began to crack.

The crack widen and got bigger and bigger until it open completely.

Exposed was a break, then the head popped out, and the beautiful feathered wings and body to reveal a baby chick humbert. Mama went out to look for food.

Humbert you would think from the first three letters of his name would normally be stereotyped as a scrooge, but humbert was just the opposite a gentle forgiving creature who had learned to control his emotions. He taught it out and rationalized the situation that in his own words "there had to be a good reason for the mistake, and if discovered Santa Clause would make it right". There was only one thing to do write a letter to Santa and send it to the North Pole.

<u>*Chapter 4 Letter to Santa*</u>

Humbert wrote:

December 10th

North Pole Workshop Office

Urgent: Attention: Santa Clause

Dear Sir,

Greetings. I hope you are doing well. By way of introduction I am Humbert Hummingbird. You can call me Hummy. I write to inform you of a little mistake your staff has made on last year. You see my friend Motlee Butterfly and I were not happy on last Christmas because we were forgotten.

We did not receive any thing for Christmas even though we did our best to be nice as boy scouts normally do. Motlee has emotional issues and is very angry about the whole affair. I suspect that he has lost faith in Christmas and Santa clause. I have tried to talk to him but to no avail, Please help.

*Hopeful for a better Christmas this year with double presents to make up for the short fall. **I still believe,***

Humbert.

The letter was emailed to Santa to get the fastest response. In minutes there came in a notification with the words" thank you for your email, I'm checking my data base and my list, and I'll check it twice. "Will get back to you as soon as possible to see if you were really naughty or nice". Santa called in the Chief Elf Xavier and arranged a meeting with his staff. In the meeting it turned out that a novice elf had written on the wrong side of the page in Santa's journal adding The Names of Humbert and Motlee to the naughty list. "I take full responsibility for it said the Chief Elf, I have already sent a letter of apology to the boys and offered them a free ride in Santa's sleigh to the North Pole. It will be a two day trip." "Their presents are being packed now as we speak"." Very good" Santa said.

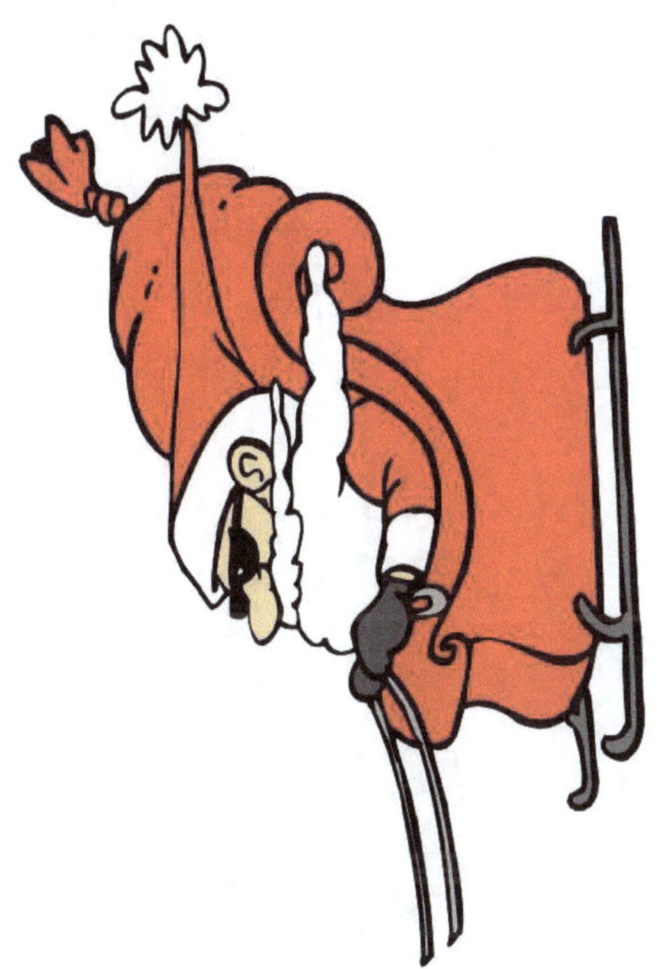

Santa Claus
North Pole

Hummy showed his friend Motley the email from the chief elf in hopes that his friend might feel better. Motlee responded "Why should I even be happy? Nothing can reverse last year's disappointment for me, I hate Santa and I hate Christmas!" "Motley said with a nasty tone in his voice, arms firmly crossed over his chest. "Something had upset him and that **one disappointment overshadowed all the other amazing things** *he had going for him: He was with his friend Humbert, whom he affectionately called Hummy. He was going to the North Pole for two days. But he got puffed up. Humbert was frustrated with how ungrateful his friend was being. But then he also realized that something else was happening here with Motley. Motley* **expected things like toys, events, activities and other people to make him happy**. *He did not know the true meaning of Christmas. "It is the season of giving! Peace on earth, good will to* men. He relied on outside forces to secure his happiness. **Because he had no clue how to find happiness within himself.**

And that's something he needed to change, quickly because going through life unhappy when you have the power to be happy is no way to live your life at all. But would he change? Anger and bitterness overwhelmed Motley who kept talking to Humbert and the more he talked his negativity the more Humbert felt the peer pressure and he finally gave in, After Motley told him if he did not do it he would not be his friend any more. The pressure became too great and Humbert cracked under it. He did not want to be alone. He wanted to stay best friends with Motley. The friends decided to formulate a nothing for Christmas revenge plan which involved playing pranks on people to make Santa look bad. They decided to put coals in the stocking to replace the real gifts. But how will they get around to do it? "I know" said Motley." "We steal Santa's sleigh on Christmas Eve night". "All we have to do is stay up late all night and when Santa goes into a nearby house, we would sneak up to the reindeers outside, bribe them with carrots and take the sleigh". "Easy as pie".

Santa arrived in the neighborhood and the two partners in crime were waiting for him to leave the sleigh. Down the chimney he went and up on the roof the two fends went. Yes it was time for payback! They took the sleigh and played a recording of Santa's voice "On Dasher, on Dancer, on Prancer, on Vixen, on Comet, on Cupid, on Donner, on Blitzen." "Now dash away, dash away, dash away all". Motley laughed. An evil, horrid sound came from his mouth, he felt like the Grinch and Ebenezer scrooge all wrapped up into one, just thinking how the plan to replace the real gifts with gift wrapped boxes that contain a lump of coal only inside was finally coming together. While Humbert started feeling guilty about the whole situation. But he did not want to offend his friend Motley. The two had reached the first house and planted the fake gifts. Motlee made sure to fill up every stocking with coal and *a note that said nothing for Christmas and signed his name Motley at the end.*

The naughty friends went from house to house repeating the evil plan. Motley and Humbert even ate some of the cookies and drinked the milk that was left for Santa. After the prank at the second house something had rubbed off from Motley to Humbert, because he too was now feeling like the Grinch and he managed to show an evil smile, then an evil laugh. They both looked at each other and evil laughter filled the air. "Ah, Ha, ha, aha, ha". Humbert did not know what came over him all of a sudden. Naughtiness was contagious. This one thing he did realize was the more he did it the more it felt really, really good. Humbert's strong conscience was telling him "You must stop this now! This is not good, you can still make the nice list." Humbert's conscience spoke even louder to him as he looked at the Christ child lying in the manger in the nativity near the fire place inside the first house.

Meanwhile Santa was communicating with his Chief Elf. "I need your help, I made a delivery at the first house and then upon my return to the roof I discovered that the sleigh was missing!

Please bring the backup automatic sleigh, right away". "We must get to the bottom of this as soon as possible." Xavier the Chief Elf used the magic fairy dust on the sleigh even though it had an electric motor and rocket trustors.

He arrived in a half hour from the North Pole, and the race was on to recover Santa's Main sleigh. But alas the two friends Humbert and Motley had done a lot of damage to Santa's reputation in that short space of time.

You see some of the children had also stayed up the night before Christmas to peek and await the arrival of Santa Clause. Some had even already opened up the stockings and found the coal inside.

What a dilemma for Santa and Christmas!

How will Santa be able to fix Christmas now? Humbert's conscience began to burn inside him. A still small voice was telling him he had done wrong.

The manager seen was etched into his mind. "Motley I Think we did enough, let's return Santa's Sleigh to the first house, where we saw him land" said Humbert." Ok then" said Motley. While they taught of this the automatic sleigh pulled upon them." Pull over" Xavier said. "Give us back the sleigh". "If you give up now just maybe, Santa Might forgive you! "We were just going back to the first house to return it" said

Motley." Ok go to the first house then and we'll sort it all out there. Said the Elf."

The Chief Elf Xavier questioned the two naughty friends. "What are your names?

"How many houses have you been to? What have you done there? Did you see any children there? Why did you do it? The friends answered"

I'm Motlee and I'm Humbert" We visited about Ten Houses, ate the cookies and drink the milk, left coal in the stockings, we did not see any children, but we did hear some noise at some of the houses.

Maybe they might have been peeking". I came up with the plan and pressured Humbert to assist me" said Motlee.

Santa spoke "Humbert I read your letter personally and answered it" promise me that you will never ever give in to peer pressure again"" I promise Santa" said Humbert.

"You are stronger than anger, Frustration, Peer pressure, fear and sadness. The control is in side both of you.

I know you will make me and children all around the world proud this Christmas. Just then a giant clock chimed the time. It was twelve O'clock.

"Oh my I have a lot of work to undo, let's get started Motlee! First an apology "Yes Santa" then you drive the sleigh to the houses were you have been and, both of you undo your work while I will do mine,

If you do this I will forgive you and make you honorary elves for life"." Do we have a deal? "Yes sir, yes sir".

"We are very, very sorry for what we did, we would not do it again, please forgive us". They said. Turning to Motlee Santa Said"

You must learn to control and manage your emotions especially your anger better." I am not saying to ignore your feelings" Feelings are the way that your body speaks to you. When you are angry. You must Stop, take a break and think about a solution to the problem that you are facing, before you act out".

"Breathe in then out slowly. Count to ten and breathe. "If an adult is around at the time that you are having a bad situation, you can talk to that adult about how you are feeling".

"Tell them what you like or dislike about the situation". "Frustration can often occur from being unable to solve a problem, experiencing a roadblock, or annoyance".

"Frustration in a child can often lead to anger and adverse reactions if one does not take caution".

"Stopping to take a break is often a great way to prevent irritation". "Think happy thoughts about an event or experience in your pass, like a happy birthday or moment in your life".

"Your Emotions matter and controlling those emotions matter even more than the emotions itself, because people who are hurting can sometimes hurt other people".

Santa continued. "When children are angry, they can manifest their anger through bad behavior".

"They might shout, cry, throw things and roll on the floor or all of these things combined".

"I understand why you threw the tantrum" Santa said." "We made a bad mistake at the North Pole for whatever reason".

"But I am sorry, Please forgive me and my staff for the blunder." "I promise you, we will make it right through restoration." "Give me the badges Xavier" Santa said.

"I hereby appoint you, honorary elves, one for you and one for you, he said as he pinned the badges on the lads".

Into the sleigh they went. Santa gave his famous command to the reindeers "Rudolph light the way! Now, Dasher! Now, Dancer! Now, Prancer and Vixen! On, Comet! On, Cupid! On, Donner and Blitzen! To the top of the porch! To the top of the wall! Now dash away! Dash away! Dash away all!"

They had arrived at the first house within minutes. They did not know that a nice little boy and girl were awoke sad and in shock.

They had witnessed what Humbert and Motley had done earlier and were debating what to do next. There was a big thump on the roof of the house.

Then the braying of reindeers. A sigh of relief came over the children as they placed the carrots for the reindeers and for Santa the cookies and milk on the chimney mantle.

"It's Santa, let's hide the two children said. Down the chimney came Santa and his little Helpers with the presents and a blast of fairy dust filled the air. Just what they kids had asked for. A Barbie doll and play station 5 game console with bonus games.

While Santa and the two little helpers worked, the children came out to talk to them. "Good night." "Why is there coal in our stockings, Santa? The children asked.

I will let my friends explain the whole thing said" Santa. Motlee and humbert told their story of being reformed from naughtiness and why they did it.

They were now working with Santa and were mending their ways undoing the bad things they had done. Santa told them not to give in to peer pressure as Humbert had done."

If someone is pressuring you to do bad things, you can tell an adult" You can say Stop, I will not do it, and I choose to do well."

"You can make new friends and refuse to hang out with bullies or be controlled by peer pressure and be miserable as a puppet on a string."

"Remember that no one has the right to make you feel powerless, miserable or uncomfortable"

"You always have a choice to do good all of the time". "Go back to bed now children said Santa." We will, but first we have replaced your cookies and milk, please accept them.

Santa thanked the children as they left for bed. Santa pointed his finger to his nose and in a flash up the chimney He went with his helpers.

Santa was now making good time in his delivery. In time all the houses around the World were visited. Santa took Motlee and Humbert to the North Pole.

At the entrance they were met by a snowman. ”Welcome, Merry Christmas.” he said. “Merry Christmas to you too, Santa and his helpers said as they walked past him to the workshop”.

Xavier chief The Elf

Chapter8 The North Pole

The North Pole was everything that Motlee and Humbert had ever dream of and more. It was beautiful amazingly better than the fairy tales in the story books. Millions of presents and candy were on conveyer belts. Elves busy making toys,

painting toys, designing and drawing toys.

Running to and fro.

There were two large books. Santa's naughty list and nice list books. Santa called Motlee and Humbert "come here and look at the nice List". The little helpers came up to the book and as they looked their names were being written before their eyes in gold ink. Wow" Said Humbert. "Yes because you undid what you did, and went beyond that". "You help me in my delivery of the presents to kids all over the world you were given gold ink instead of normal ink". "Normal ink fades eventually but gold ink last forever." "It tells me that you have done the good work from your heart genuinely. Thank you". "And now Xavier will give you a tour of the workshop". Elves were dressed in green and some in red clothing, with large, pointy ears and wearing pointy hats. Santa's elves were everywhere making the toys in Santa's workshop and doing chores taking care of his reindeers, among other tasks such as Guarding the secret location of

Santa's village and workshop; make sure that Santa's sleigh is in working order; to help Santa keep his Naughty or Nice List in order, make toys and organize them onto Santa's sleigh, keep an eye on children's behavior and report back to Santa or the chief elf who makes up the naughty list.

Mrs. Clause was cooking for Santa and His Guest. Whipping up delicious desserts exclusively available at the North Pole, She said "Hello children and welcome to the North Pole". "I hope you enjoy your stay" she said as she placed a tray of cookies on the table.

It was time to go home. Santa Humbert and Motlee left the North Pole in the sleigh. They were tired by this time and it was time to go to bed, but first Motlee wanted to get some sweet nectar into his mouth from nearby flowers. And he did get a lot. "Now off to bed with you both so that you would be fresh to meet the challenges of the coming new day. After all it would be Christmas within hours" said Santa. Santa went up the chimney to his sleigh for the ride back home.

It was morning and everything seems as if it was a dream to them but they knew that it had been very real. The elf badges were still pinned on their shirt front pocket. The two got up excited to know what their presents would be. The family sat at their beautifully decorated Christmas tree gazing at all the lights and presents. Everyone was anxious to hear the "words" you can open the presents now." The spirit of Christmas was being felt in the house. What is the spirit of Christmas, you might ask? It is in the 'togetherness of family and friends', it's in the thought to which you put into thinking about others, it's a selfless time, where we forgive, take stock of what's important and become 'better' people. Christ child the real gift to the world and the reason for the season. The family began to sing along as the Christmas carols rang out from a nearby church bell. The Christmas day *activities had begun and Everyone's faces light up as the presents were being opened.*

The End.

We can help our kids **teach and help them to learn to be happier. Teach them that happiness is a choice.** It's up to them. **How he reacts and responds to life's events, disappointments, and other people is entirely in their control.** They get to decide if something is going to crush them and ruin their day or if they are going to allow it to or search for the good in the situation. If you feel your child is clinically depressed or has mental health issues, please seek professional help. These suggestions are not intended to replace medical advice. Feeling happy, being happy at will or choosing happiness can be learned, but it takes practice. This is how to do it, practice finding happiness with the children who forget to look for the happiness. **Tell them its okay to be sad or unhappy or disappointed.** Teach kids to be happier without discounting their feelings of being sad, unhappy, or disappointed. **You don't want them to cover up their true feelings or pretend those feelings aren't there.** It's okay to be sad. But it's **not okay to be sad all the time.** It's not fun to be miserable and upset for the sake of being miserable and upset. Our **kids can decide enough is enough, the time to be sad is over**, and it's **time to choose happiness. The e**xception to the rule, of course, does not apply to deep emotional distress issues of death, illness, or abuse. **"Remind our children to focus on the happy things"** refers to "child-appropriate" dramas such as running out of their favorite granola bar, having to take turns with their favorite toy, or striking out at the baseball game. If your child is dealing with a situation tell them to **Smile or laugh to release endorphins. Smile or laugh, even when you're in pain or incredibly unhappy**, so your body will release endorphins. These endorphins will naturally make you feel better. So when someone is upset and fakes their smile or they laugh, their body will release endorphins which **naturally reduces feelings of sadness and depression**. Your body doesn't know if you're faking the smile. **Purposefully think happy thoughts:** Channel your thoughts. **Take control of your mind and think happy thoughts**. Kids can purposefully set aside sad thoughts in their minds when we remind them to **think about things that make them happy or things they're looking forward to**. Maybe they can envision their upcoming birthday party or think back to their last one. They can focus on the next holiday coming up or remember a vacation they just took. Because even in our sadness, we need to know there are things in our life that could make us happier if we **pause to take the time to think about them**. No child should ever have to deal with, anxiety, depression or deep emotions of grief by themselves.

<u>Disclaimer:</u> If you feel your child is clinically depressed or has mental health issues, please seek professional help. This is not intended to replace medical advice. Remember when bad things happen; First you stop, and Say" I'm Stronger than Anger, frustration, sadness, anxiety, grief and fear" Breathe a few times in and out slowly and think of doing something different or imagine nice things that happen in the past. Practice it often: Breathe and exhaled, then breathe, exhale and then breathe. The more you breathe it gets easier then better and better until eventually you will calmed yourself down. Good luck with your practicing being in control of your emotions. And have a very merry Christmas.

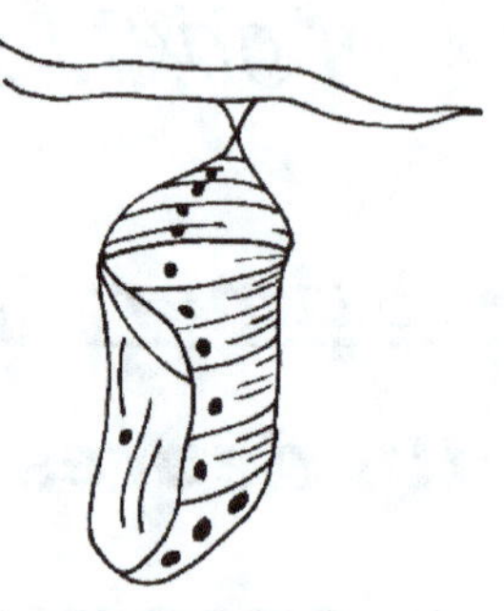

Motlee's life Cycle

Which pictur ong

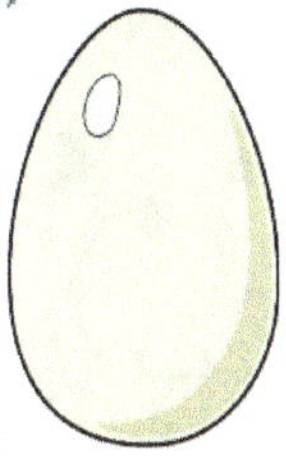

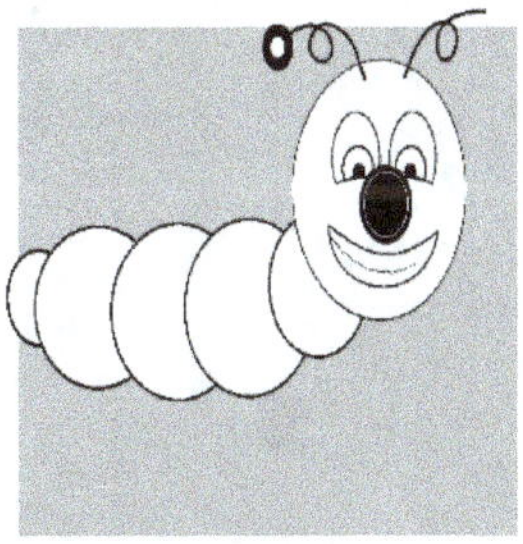

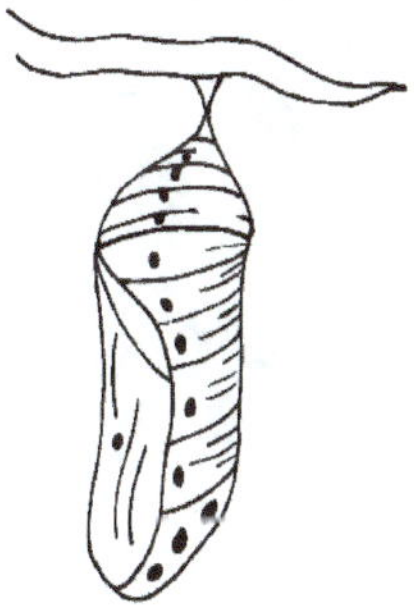

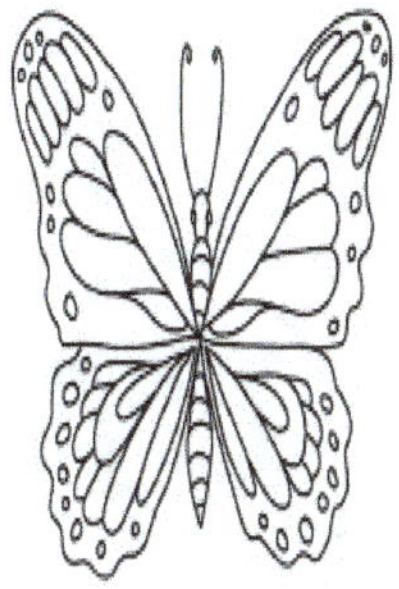

Answer: ***the bird***

Motlee had been overlooked on last Christmas by mistake. It was an oversight unforgivable in Motlee's eyes. Santa Clause is to blame because he is in charge of the gifts, the Elves, The reindeers, the sleigh, even the North Pole workshop" " I hate Christmas and I hate Santa Clause! Said Motlee. Motlee is feeling angry but what he does not know was that Santa had been sick and the delivery was made by the chief Elf instead last year. All Motlee knew was that he and his friend Hummy got nothing for Christmas. They were good but somehow they made the naughty list. Motlee's emotions are out of control. Now, Motlee, the butterfly is about to influence his friend Humbert the hummingbird to do bad things. After all, they were already on the naughty list. Motlee uses peer pressure to exert his will on his friend. This book will teach your child self-help ways on how to cope with some emotional situations.

This is Book 1 from the series Adventures of Motlee the Butterfly by Prince Albert King.

ROBERTS
DAY OF
EMOTIONS
AND
HALLOWEEN
PRINCE KING

Prince King
The Hiccup book was written for kindergarten and preschool Kids. It is made with the hopes of being interactive with the characters.
The hiccup book

THE TREASURE COAST
A TALE OF PIRATE'S TREASURE
PRINCE KING

My First Toddler Coloring Book
ACTIVITY BOOK
ANIMALS, SHAPES, ABC ,COLORS AND MORE
FOR KIDS 3-4 YEARS OLD
BY PRINCE ALBERT KING

For booking events or book signings contact:

P.O.BOX SB51712 NASSAU N.P., BAHAMAS. Telephone" 2423939410

THE
BAHAMIAN
JOHNNY
CAKE RUN
THE BAHAMIAN JOHNNYCAKE RUN 2
SECOND EDITION
PRINCE KING
PRINCE KING
PKDP
ACCOUNTING
LEDGER
JOURNAL
PKDP PRESS
PRINCE KING
The
Little
Humming
Bird
HUMBERT

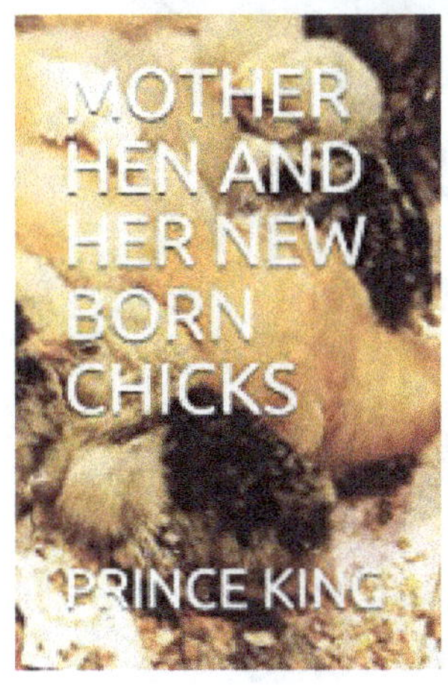
MOTHER
HEN AND
HER NEW
BORN
CHICKS
PRINCE KING

ABOUT THE AUTHOR

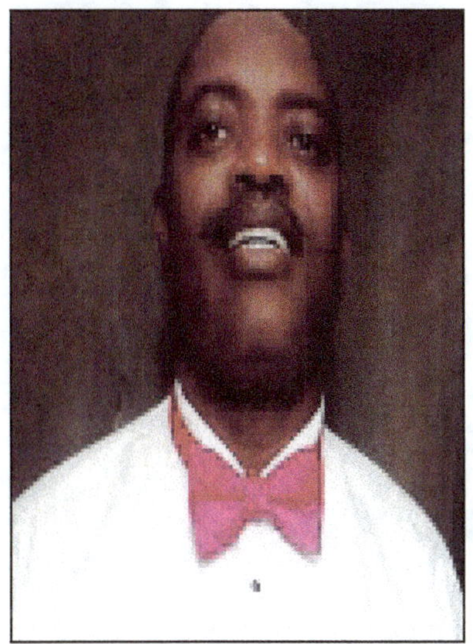

Prince Albert King lives in Nassau, Bahamas. He is married to the beautiful Samantha Wilson King. The couple has four children. The Author is a history buff and a third generation Police Officer (retired). In 2001 he founded Kingco Computer Systems and in 2018 he founded PKDP Printing Press.